When You're Going TO THE Moon

Sasha Beekman

Vivienne To

affirm press

For my mum, who always knew how far I could climb

Sasha

For Mum, for always encouraging us to dream

Vivienne

affirm press

First published by Affirm Press, 2018
This edition published by Affirm Press, 2024
Bunurong/Boon Wurrung Country
28 Thistlethwaite Street
South Melbourne VIC 3205

Affirm Press is located on the unceded land of the Bunurong/Boon Wurrung peoples of the Kulin Nation. Affirm Press pays respect to their Elders past and present.

10 9 8 7 6 5 4 3 2 1

NATIONAL LIBRARY OF AUSTRALIA

A catalogue record for this book is available from the National Library of Australia

ISBN: 9781923135888 (paperback)

Colour separation by Splitting Image Colour Studio, Clayton, Victoria

Printed and bound in China by RR Donnelley Asia Printing Solutions Ltd.

affirmpress.com.au

There's a lot you've got to fit in your little green bag

when you're going to the moon.

So empty out all the useless stuff you've got in there.

Your school books.

Lunchbox.

Calculator.

Umbrella.

You won't need any of them once you're on the moon.

Pack all your very best things into your little green bag.

Your glittery yo-yo,

your bendy soup spoon,

your yellow kazoo.

Your paint brush,

that coin you found

on the ground yesterday,

your inflatable moose.

Then pack your favourite blanket.

The one with the hole in the

shape of a boat.

You never know! It might be cold on the moon.

Done your lucky dance?

A slide.

A twirl.

A jump to the sky!

Now you’re *definitely* ready to climb really high.

Grab a ladder, the tallest you can find.

Get your balance. One step at a time.

But wait! Your tap-dancing shoes.

You can't go without those.

Come on now. You can do it.

Try not to look down.

But your pet iguana, Rochelle.

She'll want to come too!

You're all set. It's time to go . . . But the moon *is* pretty far away.

Maybe you'll need a map of the world. With a great, big 'X' to mark the spot.

Just so you know where dinner will be warm and waiting for you,

right after you're back from going to the moon.

Now you're ready. And you're sure.

And you definitely can't miss dessert.

Climb up . . .

. . . and up . . .

. . . and up.

And bit by bit, it's getting brighter.

Once you reach the moon,

when you're finally there . . .

Sit down. Unpack your little green bag.

Take a look out at all you can see.

And know that you made it.

Before you got too big.

Too big to believe you could come this far . . .

Too big to believe you really can reach the stars.